DRUGS

DRUGS

ART KAPONE
KAMDYN MOORE

Art Kapone and Kamdyn Moore

Drugs

Disclaimer

All characters, events, and entities portrayed in this book are purely fictional. Any resemblance to real persons, living or dead, or actual events is entirely coincidental. The names, places, and incidents are the product of the author's imagination and are not intended to reflect any real-world individuals, organizations, or locations.

Published by Spines Publishing Platform

ISBN: 979-8-89691-497-6

CONTENTS

CHAPTER 1

SHADOWS UNDER STATUES

The parks in Bristol, Pennsylvania, were a trap.

In the daylight, they were filled with the shouts of kids playing tag or basketball, the scrape of bikes on asphalt, and the occasional jingles of an ice cream truck—driven by undercover cops. They served ice cream while casing the block, acting like the hood didn't know.

But beneath the surface, the parks were battlegrounds. Fights broke out almost daily, fueled by grudges, drugs, boredom, and gunshots. Dealers exchanged bags for cash on the same benches where kids ate their sandwiches. Violence and innocence lived side by side.

Dru sat on the swings, watching it all unfold.

At 11, he had already seen more chaos than he thought possible. He'd seen fights turn bloody, heard gunshots shatter the night, and watched kids his age get pulled into things they didn't understand.

"Yo, Dru!"

A voice snapped him out of his thoughts.

Malik, leaning against the chain-link fence near the basketball court, waved him over. Dru hesitated, glancing at the boys playing basketball. One of them, no older than ten, was trying to handle the rock past a teenager twice his size. A shove sent the younger boy sprawling, and laughter erupted from the sidelines. Dru looked away and headed toward Malik.

Dru's home was no honeycomb hideout from the streets. The house was a battlefield in its own way, filled with the sharp sting of his mother's words and the bruising weight of his uncles' fists.

His uncles drifted in and out of their small house like stragglers, always smelling of alcohol and anger. They carried their frustrations from the bottle to Dru, using him as a punching bag when they couldn't face their own failures.

"You think you're tough, homes? Huh?" one of them slurred one night, cornering Dru in the kitchen. "Think you're better than me?"

Dru kept his head up. "This my momma house. Where yours at?"

The first punch came quick, jolting him back. The second sent him to the ground.

"Speak up!" his uncle roared, standing over him.

"I—I didn't say that," Dru pouted, his lips trembling.

"Nah mean," his uncle muttered, stumbling away. Drunk from the promethazine he just finished, with not a drop left in the bottle, his head bobbing as he barely kept his footing.

His mother never paid the situation any mind. Sometimes, she wasn't even there—out with one of her crew or locked in her bedroom. When she did see the bruises, she didn't ask questions.

"Boy, cut it out," she'd say in a sharp tone. "All that damn whining. The world don't give a fuck about you."

Fighting back the streets were no joke—run by the Terrace Dome Kings.

Dru was small for his age, and the older boys in the neighborhood took notice. They'd shove him, trip him, and mock him until the anger bottled up inside him, threatening to explode. One day, it did.

Dru was walking home from the park when three boys blocked his path.

"Where you going, little man?" one of them taunted, stepping in front of him.

"To the crib," Dru said quietly, trying to euro-step around them. The boy shoved him back. "Not so fast. What you got in your pockets?" Dru clenched his fists, adrenaline rushing.

"Nothing."

"Don't lie," another boy said, grabbing Dru by the collar. "Run them pockets."

Before Dru could think, he threw a jab, catching the boy in the jaw. The others teed off on him immediately, blows coming from all angles. He struggled to fight back.

By the time they left, Dru was bleeding and bruised, but something inside him had shifted. He'd fought back, and for once, he didn't feel like a victim.

"Damn, kid," Malik said the next day, eyeing the fresh bruises on Dru's face. "You got strolled on, huh?"

Dru nodded, trying to hide the wince as he fixed his hoodie. "We knuckled didn't have a choice."

"You always got a choice," Malik said, lighting a cigarette.

"You just gotta know when to stand your ground and when to walk away."

Malik became a mentor of sorts, showing Dru how to navigate the unspoken rules of the streets. But Malik's lessons came with a price.

"Peer Pressure"

One afternoon, he handed Dru a Philla blunt and grinned. "Here. This'll help you forget about those fights."

Dru hesitated, staring at the blunt in Malik's hand. "I don't know... you tripping, cuz."

"Booo, it's just weed," Malik said, almost teasing. "You be cool. Better recognize—it's hard out here. You gotta learn the **aura** and get the flow of life. Get fried."

Dru's heart pounded as he took the blunt.

Locked in his room, barricaded against his uncles, Dru took his first hit.

Immediately, he felt it—his body easing, his mind drifting. The psychedelic pictures on his walls seemed to move, the glow of his lava lamp pulsing in rhythm with his heartbeat.

Fried off the first puff, he thought to himself, I could get used to this—a Kool-Aid smile stretching across his face.

The warmth that followed dulled the ache in his chest and the weight on his shoulders. For the first time in a long time, Dru felt free.

He finally got the peace of mind he had been crying for. He could breathe.

Dru woke up the next morning still feeling amazing, the euphoria from last night's blunt lingering.

Dressed fly, he wandered down Mill Street to the wharf,

staring through the windows of the retail shops. His favorite was the magic store.

Inside, an old man—the "**Magic Man**"—always had tricks to show Dru. Sleight of hand, illusions, mind games. The tricks confused him at first, but over time, they broadened his mind, leading him to a deeper understanding of things beyond the streets.

The lessons wrapped around him like a mission, their sharp realities reminding him of everything he wasn't.

For a moment, Dru let himself imagine what it would be like to matter—to have people look up to him the way the Magic Man made them believe in **illusions**.

"I'll get there," he whispered to himself.

He scratched his head, pondering. I don't know how, but I'll get there.

The vision faded as quickly as it came, replaced by the reality of bruises, empty pockets, and a growing hunger for something stronger than a blunt to take the pain away.

That feeling—the emptiness—stayed with him.

It was the first flicker of hope in a world that seemed determined to make him thug it out. To do the right thing, even when it was uncomfortable.

CHAPTER 2

FIRST BETRAYAL

It was a snowy day in the hood at Dru's grandma's house. No snowmen were being made, just a regular day where drinks, food, and narcotics were being sold. We ran a hole-in-the-wall bar provided by Section 8 housing when a knock hit the door. It wasn't a trap—it was Dru's biological father.

Dru didn't question it when his mother told him Terrence was his father. He loved this man. It was all he knew. That was Dru's Daddy. They played ball together, and he taught him how to be royal at a young age. It wasn't like he had any reason not to believe her. Terrence was the man who put the time in.

"It was seven of us," said Dru.

Terrence was the man who called the shots and prepared well-thought-out meals—from pig feet to oxtails, curry goat, red snapper, and fungi. That was a favorite dish. On occasion, he threw a football in my direction and took me to play hoops, teaching me how to fundamentally shoot a foul shot—while throwing slick comments about Shaq.

"If Shaq can make a foul shot, you better make ten," he'd say.

That was the best pastime when he was in a rare good mood. Dru didn't know what fathers were supposed to be like, but he figured this must be dat feel—distant, angry, and unpredictable. Dat feel still felt whole. He provided life lessons and structure.

He wanted to please Terrence, even when it felt impossible. He tried to keep his grades up, bringing home straight A's and certificates from school. He also learned responsibility, did chores without being asked.

Sometimes, Terrence would slide him a pound for allowance. But no matter what he did, Terrence's approval always seemed just out of reach. He had royal standards Dru still couldn't understand. Terrence originated from St. Jose Van Dykes, so he was different.

When the knock hit the door, the mood went stale. The crap games paused, the music stopped, and heads turned like the reaper had walked in. No more parlaying (partying). When Dru saw a man who looked like him, he started scratching his head in utter shock.

Dru said, "Who you?"

He played doorman from time to time at his grandma's house, securing safety.

The man responded, "I am your father."

Dru's world was instantly torn. DAT FEEL when trust was broken between everyone who knew the truth and hid it from him. Dru's mother had been accustomed to telling white lies to him his whole life.

Oppression.

His mother told him Terrence wasn't his real father.

"What?" Dru asked, staring at her as she lit a cigarette at the kitchen

table.

"I said Terrence isn't your dad," she repeated, blowing out a puff of smoke.

Dru's mouth opened, then closed. "Then who is?"

She sighed, leaning back in her chair. "Your real dad's been in federal prison. He's out on furlough now, and he wants to see you."

The words hit Dru like a smack to the back of the head from Kid 'n Play. Terrence wasn't his real dad, but that's all he knew. All the times he'd tried to earn his approval, all the hurtful words and cold shoulders—it had all been for nothing. Or at least, that's how he felt.

Dru was smart enough not to question his mother. She was powerful. He had to accept the situation but did not understand why he wasn't told sooner. Dru pondered in disbelief.

Noticing Dru's reaction, she took another puff of the cigarette, blew out smoke, and said, "I didn't see the point."

His mother shrugged. "Terrence was here, and your real dad wasn't. What difference does it make? Go hang with your father," she said.

Just that fast, Dru was forced to handle a situation without proper understanding. He stared at her, his hands balling into fists under the table. He whispered to himself, "It makes a difference to me."

She sighed again, clearly growing impatient. "Look, it doesn't matter now. He's out, and he wants to meet you. That's a good thing, isn't it?"

At that moment, Dru put his heart in a stranger's hand—known as his biological father. Dru didn't answer. His mind was spinning too fast, jumping between anger, confusion, and a little bit of hope. His real dad wanted to meet him. Maybe that meant something. Maybe it would be different this time.

The snow was falling thick and steady that day, covering the streets of Bristol—also known as Venice Ashby—in a soft, muffling white blanket. Dru and his brothers set off to hang with their (**pop**), a father that sometimes his position.

Hopping in his pop's red truck, the playlist was odd—50 Cent's Many Men, followed by Snoop Dogg's Gin and Juice. Dru began to notice things about his father that were similar to his own traits. It lightened the situation a lot.

Dru was asked, "Where do you wanna go? I don't got much cheese now," his father said.

Nervous not to set the bar too high, Dru responded, "I'd love to go skating at Cornwells Heights. All the girls be on me."

Arriving at the skate rink, Dru was escorted by his skate-rink sweetheart, Ariana. Dru introduced her to his pops, and she couldn't help but notice his features. As described, a tall man stepped forward—broad shoulders, matching facial features, wearing an Iceberg blue jean outfit with a Kangol hat.

Dru and Ariana went out, and it was time for couples to skate. While chopping it up, she opened up about Dru's emotions, meeting his father for the first time, and gave him words of encouragement. Dru wholeheartedly accepted his long-lost father.

Ariana continued holding his hand while skating to Justin Timberlake's It's Gonna Be Me. Holding her closely, trying not to fall but still wanting to be smooth for his father, Dru showed off his stuff—making his pop a proud father in that moment.

While not being able to afford some food, Ariana bought Dru something to eat. He had a way with the ladies. **Pop** drew a big grin on his face. Dru's brother looked jealous, but he paid it no mind. Dru glanced up at Ariana, his excitement star-gazed by her beauty. She was happy for Dru meeting his father.

Now it was time for shufflers.

"If you are not an advanced skater, please exit the floor," said the DJ.

As advanced as Dru was, he got out there, shuffling to When I Hear Music by Debbie Deb, freestyling his moves while showing off to his pops and Ariana—keeping up with the flow of traffic.

The Cornwells Heights skating rink was a ritual for Dru and his crew. It was the only place kids could go, their safe haven from the hood. It was peaceful, full of bliss—until they split the five hours.

For three hours, they skated. For two hours, they danced. That turned the capacity of people to the max level, bringing in all the different neighborhoods—even out-of-town cats. Dru would run amok, repping Da Terrace, bringing leadership and personality that everyone either loved or hated.

He would flirt with all the bunnies while already being locked in on one shawty, causing them to throw hands over puppy love. Dru couldn't believe what he was experiencing at the rink. They turned it from a peaceful place—then shots rang out.

Now it was a hole in the wall.
People scattered, screaming.
Dat feel from screeching wheels and gunfire was real.

Folks tried to scatter. All we heard was clatter.
I'm looking confused, like, What's the matter?
Man down—his soul shattered.
Those fun days at the rink just crippled into disbelief.
It was no longer a safe haven.
It was now dueld by streets.
By the age of sixteen, they closed it down and built a school.
Sorry. In a trance, Dru rambled a wry thought.
Ending the first night Dru met his father, it was all joy, laughs, and giggles.
We went to the Ramada Inn, and that's when the real fun started.

CHAPTER 3

PRETEEN VULNERABILITY

School had always been a source of pain for Dru. The teasing never seemed to stop. His shoes, with holes so big you could see his socks, became a running joke. His hand-me-down clothes, often too tight or too big, only made him feel more out of place.

"Yo, Dru, you got holes in them shoes, and they smell like wet dog! Fuck outta here!" one boy laughed during lunch, drawing attention to Dru's feet.

The laughter echoed in Dru's ears as he hunched over his tray, trying to make himself invisible. He never fought back; he just swallowed the hurt and let it simmer inside him. He felt invisible, even to the teachers.

No one seemed to care why his grades were slipping or why he stopped turning in homework. He wanted to yell, to tell them that it wasn't laziness—it was the chaos at home, the sleepless nights, the overwhelming sadness he couldn't shake.

As things spiralled out of control, Dru started hearing voices in his head. They were insinuating that he hurt himself or someone else.

Dru's homegirl was going on a camping trip and needed a knife. To help, Dru brought the knife to school. At random, with all the kids playing in the schoolyard, Dru just clutched the knife and started chasing people.

The first victim, Dru poked at but withdrew his knife. The second victim, Dru put the knife around their neck, resting on their Adam's apple, but again, he withdrew his knife. With the last victim, Dru took another stab, but sure not pierce flesh —all while smiling.

This was right after the Virginia Tech killings, mind you, so the stakes were really high. Consciously thinking, Dru withdrew from attacking, but part of him still wanted to hurt innocent people. Could it have been from all the chaos he had endured from his mom's negligence? Or his pop's lack of leadership, teaching him all the wrong things?

Moments later, the school bell rang, sending the kids scurrying to their homeroom doors. While attendance was being taken, the loudspeaker chimed in, calling Dru to the principal's office. Dru's heart started pumping out of his chest. He was no longer smiling.

Approaching the office, he saw the police sitting there. They started asking questions about the incident. A young Dru, at the age of 11, knew enough to understand that the cops couldn't question him without his mom present. He contested, demanding they get his mother there.

When they searched Dru, he had no knife—he had already passed it off to his friend after the incident. The crazy thing about this? Dru got snitched on. Not by the victims, but by an eyewitness. She got expelled. They found the knife on her.

They sent Dru to the police station to process him for booking. Dru was sent to **Bucks County Youth Center**, where he would proceed to fight his case.

Surprisingly, the environment lifted a lot of weight off Dru's shoulders. There, he was treated with dignity and respect. Well-fed, he politicked with other kids, learning that he wasn't the only one experiencing the voices that had taken hold of him due to anger and the negligence of bad parenting.

During lock-up, Dru began eating better and started healing from his horrid childhood.

On the outside, Dru's mom was devastated. She felt like she had driven her son to snap. She invested in the top lawyer to get him some justice. The charges that stood were possession of a deadly weapon in a school zone.

Dru did 30 days with indefinite probation, meaning he would be released from it at 18. He was required to attend the Neighborhood First Program.

Dru got a chance to forgive himself during that time. He wasn't fully healed, but he was learning to accept himself. He played basketball, read books, and played cards. Group therapy was mandatory for every client at the youth center.

Thirty days went by, and Dru touched down back in his hood. It felt different. He was no longer going to the same school; his routines had changed. He was sent to an alternative school called Middle Earth, a place for students the system had deemed too "**difficult**" to manage.

There, the curriculum was different—it focused on creative thinking, artisanal skills, and life lessons. While Dru still ran into even more troubled kids, he would end up in fights. One fight led to Dru breaking a kid's nose, setting the tone for himself. He gained respect from the rest of his fellow classmates.

The transition was jarring. The alternative school was smaller and quieter, but it wasn't just the building that was different—it was the people. The teachers didn't see Dru as a problem to be fixed. They saw him as a kid with potential.

One of those teachers was Mr. Henderson, who taught life skills. He had a way of talking to Dru that didn't make him feel judged.

"You've got something special in you, Dru," he told him one day. "I can see it. Now you just have to see it too."

Science was a major focus at the alternative school, and Dru loved it. The school helped Dru overcome his shyness. One day, Mr. Henderson assigned an oral report. Each student had to speak for 10 minutes about their favorite hero in the world.

Dru felt a pang of panic at first—public speaking wasn't something he wanted to do. As he thought about the assignment, one name came to mind: **Martin Luther King Jr.**

Dru had learned about King before, but it wasn't until he started researching for his report that he truly understood the man's impact. He read about King's courage, his vision, and his unwavering commitment to **peace** and **justice**, even in the face of **violence** and **hatred.**

On the day of his presentation, Dru stood at the front of the class, his hands trembling as he held his notes. But as he started speaking, something shifted.

"Martin Luther King wasn't just a leader," Dru began, his voice gaining strength. "He was someone who believed in change, even when it seemed impossible. He didn't fight back with violence—he used words, ideas, and love."

Dru spoke about King's dream of equality, his marches for **civil rights**, and his belief in the power of peaceful resistance. As he talked, Dru felt a flicker of something he hadn't felt in a long time: hope.

When he finished, the class clapped, and Mr. Henderson smiled warmly.

"That was powerful, Dru," he said. "You've got a voice, and it's worth hearing."

The research and presentation planted a seed in Dru's mind. For so long, he had believed that the only way to survive was to fight, to harden himself against the world. But King's story showed him a different way—a way to channel his anger and pain into something meaningful.

"I never thought about it like that before," Dru admitted to Mr. Henderson after class. "Using words instead of fists."

Mr. Henderson nodded. "Words can be just as powerful as actions, Dru. Sometimes even more so."

The lesson stayed with him. For the first time, Dru began to think about what kind of person he wanted to be—not just for himself, but for the world around him.

Outside of school, Dru continued to attend the Neighborhood First Program. At first, it felt like just another obligation, but over time, the program became a refuge. The staff treated Dru with respect and patience, helping him unpack the emotions he'd buried for so long.

"**You're not alone in this**, Dru," Mr. Carter, his counselor, told him during one of their sessions. "We've got your back, but you gotta meet us halfway."

Neighborhood First combined counseling, life skills, and creative outlets like art and writing. Dru found himself drawn to the art room, where he could lose himself in sketches and paintings. **Art** became his way of processing emotions he couldn't put into words.

Dru was beginning to change. For the first time in his life, he realized that maybe—just maybe—he could be something more than what the streets had planned for him.

CHAPTER 4

THE HIGH PRICE OF ESCAPE

As Dru grew older, the streets called to him with a hold he couldn't resist. Despite the lessons he'd learned at **Neighborhood First** and the structure provided by the alternative school, the streets offered something those places couldn't: belonging. Malik and his crew were Dru's family, the only people who seemed to understand him without asking questions.

"You're one of us," Malik often said, slapping Dru on the back with a grin. "We gotta take our own control."

For Dru, that sense of power was exclusive. Malik wasn't just his best friend—he was his brother, his protector. But the streets didn't give anything for free. **Loyalty** came with a price, and Dru was about to pay it.

One night, Malik invited Dru to a parlay at the homie's crib. The apartment was just a few dudes. The homie had a sister Dru liked, so he didn't mind the crew being there. The music in the background was So Sick by Benefit. They had just caught a major lick—now it was time to bust down the earnings. They had just gone around town snorting cocaine and checking car doors.

That's when Dru hit a jackpot on his third vehicle—a cooler full of beer, an ounce of cocaine, an ounce of weed, and a console full of quarters.

Dru hollered, "**Jackpot**!" to the crew.

They regrouped, masked up with gloves on. They went to the rendezvous to break down the earnings, while Malik's only focus was to stay high. He couldn't cope with the fact that his parents had split up and that he had to bounce back and forth between his mom's and dad's houses. He proceeded to take the coke and baking soda, pulled out a spoon, a cap full of water, and started cooking.

Dru, not understanding that method of using cocaine—all he knew was snorting—watched as Malik finished his "**science project.**" What appeared was a rock of cocaine.

The crew pushed Dru to overcome his **fear**. Malik then pulled out a pipe, stuffed it with some kind of filter, and lit it. He took a hit, got stuck with a huge smile, and then said, "Now your turn. The whole crew gotta try."

The weight of the room's expectations pressed down on Dru. He didn't want to seem **weak**, especially not in front of Malik.

Anyway, he took the pipe and inhaled.

The **rush** was immediate—a wave of **euphoria** that erased every **worry**, every **doubt**, every ounce of **pain**. We passed around the ooouuwap (crack pipe). The room began to shift, as well as the crew's thoughts.

But as the high faded, Dru felt something darker creeping in—a hunger he couldn't explain. He didn't realize it then, but that one hit was the beginning of a downward spiral that would consume him.

Dru started breaking down the weed, adding the rest of the cooked coke, crushing it into the blunt, creating a wu blunt. Dru thought he had just found a new way to cope.

"See?" Malik said, laughing. "Told you it'd **change** your life."

The parties became a regular part of Dru's life. He would crash every party he saw—even if he was uninvited. He was the party crasher. It didn't matter whose hood he was in, he was that kid—everybody accepted him.

One night, the crew crashed a party at the Days Inn hotel. It was hosted by a man from the town who was no longer alive. He pulled out a crack pipe—he was stocked up with an ounce of crack. He appeared to be an OG, so Dru and the crew were accepting of his energy.

The dimly lit, smoke-filled room reeked of addiction. Porn played on the TV screen. Pipes filled with crack. Malik was in heaven. It was a way to escape for the night from our parents. They thought we were at Malik's crib watching movies.

"I don't feel right, cuz," said Dru.

Malik, fried and stuck like Chuck, grinned and muttered, "**DAT FEEL.**"

It was scary but funny. We were overdosing on cocaine by the hit—we had taken too many hits.

The OG waited until we were so high—then he pulled out his **GAT** (penis) and started stroking it.

Dru thought, "What the fuck?"

"**Old head, you wildin'**," snarled Dru.

That's when Dru realized that Malik's addiction had put the crew in a sticky situation.

The OG had a gun. Dru knew it. To **survive**, Dru went along with it.

DAT FEEL was weird. Dru was forced to rub his GAT while smoking crack. Dru didn't sleep. He was thinking of a plan every second the situation prolonged.

Dru knew the only exit was to comply or **retaliate**. There were no locked doors, but the coke had locked our minds up, leaving us helpless to defend ourselves. That OG is no longer alive—**RIP**.

Dru couldn't call for help. They had been **lured** to what appeared to be a party.

"It turned into survival mode."

The crew made it out, vowing never to talk about that story again. It changed us all, leaving us **self-conscious** about the way we looked at our OGs. From that point on, the crew survived. Dru became a boss—a leader of the crew. He no longer followed.

Following the days after, Malik spiraled out of control, changing his **addiction** to OxyContin 80 mg. He branched off, got a new crew, and came up.

They also introduced Dru to a new scheme—**manipulating** the bank for thousands of dollars a day to get high for free.

Malik was no ordinary addict now—he had mastered a way to get high daily without working, robbing, or stealing. He just knew the banking system.

Eventually, Malik got locked up and joined a white racial gang for protection—the **Aryan Brotherhood**—which gave him a different outlook on life. Malik now hated everything, everyone, and even himself.

When Malik got out, he appeared normal—like the same old

Malik. During their reunion, Malik, fresh out, suggested that they catch one last lick.

"It's time to turn a new leaf."

Dru was always loyal to Malik—they fed each other and had a tight connection.

They caught a lick—eight PlayStation 3s. It was a fast, clean job. No guns, no tires screeching—just a well-thought-out process.

As they slid off, Malik drove. He suggested they go get some bud for the rendezvous. He knew Dru wasn't into catching licks just to get high on hard drugs. Dru, still in a euphoria from the lick, said,

"Aight."

They stopped at the bud man's house. Dru got out.

The moment he stepped inside, Malik and his girl sped off. When Dru came back out, he noticed Malik had pulled off.

Dru, shaking his head, muttered, "Oh hell nah," in his best Smokey voice.

Had they really pulled off on him?

Thinking on his toes, Dru knew he had just gotten beat.

Dru called his shawty. She came through immediately. They approached

Malik's house—his dad wasn't home.

Dru didn't knock. He knew Malik was doped out, asleep.

On account of the loss Dru had just taken, he broke in through the window. He found Malik and his chick knocked out off the dope.

Dru went in **solo** while they slept—cleaned the house out, taking back six PlayStation 3s. Malik had already sold two that fast—it pissed Dru off. He cleared the house, taking alcohol from the bar, food, cash, and valuables.

Just because he knew Malik would know who did it. Dru just sent a message.

And then, he rolled out. Casually.

CHAPTER 5
THE WEB OF LOVE AND GUILT

Dru's double life put him in situations where the outcome was unpredictable. Dru and his brother had just caught another kick for 400 **methadone** and 300 **Xanax** pills. Dru's brother passed him a gun for the jam. Dru wasn't a fan of guns, so he wiped it down, stashed it, and showed his older brothers how to take a lick without using one.

After Dru got the pack, he immediately turned it into **cash**, selling 400 methadone pills for $10 a pop. He loved Xanax, so he just ate them over time. Adding them to his Hawaiian Punch was his favorite **concoction**. He would black out immediately.

"Crime sprees came about!"

Dru had a side chick while he was married, so he and his brother shot out to the city to kick it with her. The situation escalated quickly when they missed the last train and got stuck down in West Philly down bottom, with Dru's pockets stuffed with cash. They went to the **PIC**, a hole-in-the-wall strip joint, to kill time until the train came. Leaving the club Dru and his crew was setup during a large purchase of drugs. It turn violent. They lived to tell the story. Now Dru has to go home to his wife to explain the scars and him being **M I A.**

At this time, Dru was committing **adultery**, showing no loyalty to his wife. The **drugs** and the **lifestyle** were catching up to him, causing a separation. After his marriage ended in a bitter divorce, he found himself **trapped** in a familiar cycle of despair.

Fatherhood weighed heavily on him, but so did his addiction and unresolved traumas. Feeling lost, Dru turned to dating sites for comfort, seeking a connection that could provide relief from his pain. He gravitated toward older women—**cougars**, as he called them—whose nurturing nature reminded him of the motherly love he had always craved but never fully received. These women gave Dru a place to stay, fed him, and offered stability that he didn't know how to create for himself.

Prior to his divorce, Dru had met a cougar from a dating site in the Bronx. She appeared to be a **catfish**—she looked nothing like her pictures. But Dru had just driven from Bensalem, PA, so he wasn't about to turn back. She got in the car, and they went to get the party favorites—Corona and an ounce of weed, which she bought for him. She also got the hotel room.

Once they got situated, Dru remembered her cracking open the beers. The next thing he knew, he took a sip and **date raped**, started fading like never before. A strange, overwhelming sensation took over. Did she just drug me?

The next morning, Dru woke up **groggy**, his body feeling heavy. The first thing he heard was her voice, laughing. He was rapping the song Molly by Tyga and smirking.

"That's not for you, Papi," she said casually. "You was mad saucy last night."

Dru's stomach twisted. She had just admitted her **guilt**—she had drugged him, hoping for a good time. A rush of fear shot through him. He was in survival mode now. His only thought was: Make it back to my family. Now he wants to be a father 🙄

Somehow, he managed to slide out of there safely. But that wasn't the end of his internet dating experiences—it was just the beginning.

Dru later met another cougar in his own town. He helped raise her kids, taking on the role of a partner and father figure. At first, the stability felt comforting, almost like a fresh start. But the chaos that followed Dru like a shadow eventually turned the situation into turmoil. No matter how much these women gave, his unresolved pain and guilt always resurfaced, **sabotaging** what could have been stability.

Dru was yearning for fatherly love—that feeling of DATFEEL —but at the same time, he couldn't bear to accept his own absence from his children's lives.

Among the women Dru met, one stood out. She was unlike anyone else he had **encountered**—steady, patient, and deeply empathetic. Dru described her as "**Charlotte's Web**," weaving a net of **love** and support that held him together when he was at his most **fragile**.

"She made me **shine** when I wanted to **die**," Dru later reflected. "She gave me space to **breathe**, to think, and to feel again. With her, I could imagine a version of myself that wasn't broken."

Their connection was immediate, but what set her apart was her ability to look beyond Dru's mistakes and see the potential he carried. She didn't try to fix him, nor did she judge him. Instead, she offered love that was unconditional and unwavering.

With her, Dru learned what it meant to **slow down**. She showed him that life didn't have to be a constant race to **escape** pain. Instead, it could be lived moment by moment, with intention and **care**.

"She stayed down for me through everything,"

Dru wrote.

"She showed me that I was worth the effort, even when I didn't believe it myself."

This woman encouraged Dru to reflect on his life and his choices. For the first time, he began to think about being a better man—not just for her, but for himself. The years of turmoil they spent together, marked by both highs and lows, gave Dru a glimpse of what life could be if he allowed himself to heal.

Dru was looking for someone—or something—to save his life. When things didn't work out with the mothers of his children, it created a major separation he couldn't understand. The pain became unbearable. **Suicide** became an **option**. His mind spiraled out of control as his crack habit worsened. He cried for help.

One of the most transformative parts of their relationship was how she allowed Dru to be a father to her children. He helped them with homework, taught them life lessons, and played the role of a parent in ways he had always dreamed of.

For Dru, this was everything—being a father, nurturing, guiding young lives. But with this joy came unbearable guilt. Every time he looked into her children's eyes, he was reminded of his own—the ones he had left behind. The ones he had failed to be there for.

"How could I father someone else's kids," Dru often wondered, "when I wasn't there for my own?"

The guilt gnawed at him, making it harder to fully embrace the life they were building together. No matter how much love he gave to her children, it never felt like enough to make up for his absence in his own children's lives.

As the years passed, the tension between Dru's guilt and his desire to be a better man grew too heavy to bear. He loved her deeply, but the weight of his unresolved emotions and his fear of failure ultimately pushed him to make a difficult decision.

"I didn't leave because I didn't love her,"

Dru later wrote.

"I left because I loved her too much to let my brokenness destroy what she had built."

Leaving was one of the hardest things Dru had ever done. He didn't want to hurt her or her children, but he felt he couldn't continue living a lie. As he packed his bags, he thought about everything she had given him—the love, the lessons, the hope for a better future.

Though Dru returned to the streets, he carried the lessons she had taught him. Her influence stayed with him, guiding his decisions and helping him navigate the challenges of his life. She had shown him the power of patience, the value of slowing down, and the importance of facing life with an open heart.

"She taught me that slowing down isn't a weakness," Dru reflected. "It's a **strength**. It's how you find **clarity** when the world feels like it's spinning out of **control**."

Even as Dru faced the chaos of the streets again, her love served as a foundation for the changes he would eventually make in his life.

She, too, was in **SMART Recovery**, a transformative method for moving away from addictive substances and negative behaviors toward a life of positive self-regard and willingness to change. Dru, however, didn't believe in the rooms of **NA** or **AA**. It wasn't a diss toward the programs—he just couldn't see how repeatedly telling himself he was an addict or alcoholic would help him change his reservations.

Years later, Dru would look back on his time with her as one of the most **pivotal** periods of his life. She wasn't just a chapter in his story—she was a turning point. A reminder that even in the darkest times, love and patience could light the way forward.

$In his journal, he wrote:$

"She gave me love when I didn't think I deserved it. She taught me how to slow down and see the world for what it is, not what I was running from. And even though I left, I took her lessons with me."

Born in the '80s, crack baby's—
Brain chemically imbalanced,
the pack raised me.

to extortion,
women having abortions
For the thought of needing one more.
Blessed with a modern way of living,
We doctor ourselves,
prescribing our own prescriptions, with
No description of a proper dose—
We OD, if not, we die slow.
We get older but don't grow,
Regressive state of mind
In a depressive day and time.
No sexual drive,
no motivation to monopolize,
Yet we still reside,
fighting for another hit.
We conceal massive beasts,
self-medicate
To try and keep them asleep
While the government capitalizes.
Freebase will speed you to the afterlife,
Walking mummified—zombie apocalypse.
No critique,
but the meth ain't venting y'allllllll man,
Smoking out of lightbulbs will dim your lightbulbs—
No pun intended.
Misunderstood how, we as a nation can OD—
That's drugs to shopping and caffeine,
Don't forget about the sugar cane
Red 40.
No gunpowder,

but the clatter can alter
The mind of the youth—
change your life patterns
forcing us to grow from seedless root
thats a pigeon in a coup
or some pigs you wanna shoot
taking dirty money turn it clean that's a
1099 to chime the credit route
swiper the fox , awe man , that's a credit jam
400 degrees from dem backstreets
Pushed the FICO now trans union them ties
that's a 730 to equity, facts
thats caveman fries
as a burger delight
we wasn't bread right,
lost in trap across the world
chasing diamonds but only getting rocks
Old heads sat'eem down gave'eem pearls
he brought it back to change game DAT FEEL
thats devour.

CHAPTER 6

A NEW PERSPECTIVE IN A DARK PLACE

Fourth Avenue was a world of its own. The towering walls, the ever- watchful guards, and the unspoken rules of survival shaped every moment. Dru quickly learned that **respect** was currency, and **perception** was everything. Despite his past struggles, he carried himself with an air of **intelligence** and **adaptability** that earned him a place among those who ruled the block.

Nicknamed "**Blank Man**" for his resourceful ways, Dru observed the political landscape of jail life. Every race had its own structure, and **alliances** were built on unspoken agreements rather than trust.

He spent his time studying—reading law books, dissecting financial strategies, and mapping out his next move.

In the silence of his cell, Dru reflected on his journey. Every hardship, every failure, and every loss had led him here. But he refused to believe that a jail cell was his final destination.

Dru lived in a hotel while working for a Russian family-owned car dealership. The Russians saw the pain in Dru while giving him an outlet to express his creativity. Dru became an undercarriage specialist; his job was to restore the undercarriage by removing rust and patching weak spots in the frame using a compound.

Dru's crack habit was finally fed again. He hustled hard, preparing cars for his team. Dru was spiraling out of control with his habit, but he was efficient in producing excellent work. While the Russians saw the pain in his eyes during his three years there, they accepted Dru as family.

Having a fallout with his own family and holding his ground, they respected Dru.

"You have an aura that just rubs off on people," the boss would say.

Dru broke the record for the most cars painted in a single year. They loved him. But Dru lost his back working so hard. That's when crack stopped. Dru couldn't get out of bed for about a month. While maintaining the bills, he started to learn how to save.

Dru never went back to work with the Russians, but he rebuilt his own back—one day at a time. The time in the hotel came to an end, and Dru contemplated going to his mom's house to reset his mindset.

Dru stepped off the plane in North Carolina with hope and hesitation. It had been years since he'd seen his mother, and though he longed to reconnect, the weight of their past disagreements hung heavily over him. He had changed in ways that even he didn't fully understand. **Sobriety** had brought clarity, but it also forced him to face the **wreckage** he'd left behind.

His mother greeted him with a guarded smile, a mix of love

and wariness in her eyes. As they embraced, Dru felt the distance between them— **emotional**, not **physical**. She no longer knew the man he had become, and he couldn't blame her. The years apart, filled with broken promises and **chaos**, had left **scars** on both sides. Their conversations were strained.

She watched Dru like a hawk, making him leave the house when she wasn't there. He would go to the library in hopes of figuring out his next move.

When Dru shared his **dreams** of **investing** and **building** a **business**, his mother shook her head.

"You can't do this," she said, her **tone** more fearful than dismissive. "You need a real job—something stable."

But Dru wasn't deterred. He had spent hours **devouring** books, online courses, and videos about investing. He'd taught himself the **basics** of the stock market and believed he could turn his life around.

Despite her doubts, Dru made his first investment, watching the market with a mix of excitement and anxiety. The stock market brought logical understanding, helping Dru overcome his ignorance of financial literacy. It brought emotional and logical balance.

When Dru lost $1,000 in the market, it stung more than he expected. That money represented not just financial loss, but a blow to his newfound confidence. For a moment, he considered giving up, but something inside him refused to let go.

"Failure isn't the end," he told himself. "It's just part of the process."

Dru's **determination** baffled his mother. She couldn't understand why he wouldn't take a safer path, especially when he was already struggling to find steady work. Their arguments grew more frequent and heated, culminating in a confrontation that brought years of frustration to the surface.

"I'm not that little boy you once knew, Ma! Life changed me!" Dru shouted

"And I don't know who you are now," his mother replied, her voice trembling. "You say you've changed, but all I see is the same boy making mistakes."

The fight ended with the police being called—a moment Dru never imagined would happen with his own mother. Though he left willingly, the pain of their broken relationship cut deep.

Dru's journey took him to Philadelphia, where he stayed briefly with his child's mother. Their reunion was no smoother than the one with his mother, ending in a heated argument that pushed Dru back onto the streets. From there, he headed to Miami, hoping for a fresh start.

The streets of Miami were unforgiving, but Dru found solace in the **rhythm** of the city. Sleeping outside government buildings and under palm trees, he began to embrace his **homelessness** in an unexpected way.

"The power that flows outside is healing in the weirdest way," he reflected.

Each night, as the world around him slowed, Dru felt a sense of clarity he hadn't experienced before. It was **self-reliance**.

During this time, the stock market became his **anchor**. He used public Wi- Fi at libraries and cafés to track his investments, studying trends and learning from his mistakes. The market taught him **discipline**, **logic**, and **patience**—skills he began applying to other areas of his **life**.

At this time, Dru experienced **four quarters**, changing his investment strategies. He added ten dollars, purchasing penny stocks—buying in the **red,** selling in the **green**. A little bit of shares at a time. Seeing small earnings, even less than a penny, gave him the **confidence** to keep going. After he established a **balance**, he **diversified** his **portfolio**, understanding all the **entities**.

Dru began traveling across America, pulling out small wins at a time.

Dru's travels took him across the country, each stop adding new layers to his journey. In Portland, he slept in one of the city's deadliest homeless camps (**The Pit**), learning the unspoken rules of survival. The camp was a microcosm of society's struggles, filled with people battling their own **demons**. Dru found himself both a participant and an observer, absorbing wisdom from those who had lived on the streets far longer than he had. They had tents with t.v's, generators, cars ,and grills they ate well.

In Washington, Dru met strangers who restored his **faith** in **humanity**. One encounter stood out—a woman who had been **exploited** and stranded far from home. Using what little he had, Dru helped her return to Portland—an act of kindness that reminded him of his own capacity for good.

Denver offered Dru a brief respite from the chaos. Upon arriving, he called a program that provided sober living accommodations. Though the environment wasn't ideal—filled with people he didn't fully connect with— it gave Dru a sense of **stability** he hadn't felt in years. For the first time, he began to see a path forward, even if it was still hazy.

But his stay in Denver was short-lived. The **challenges** of maintaining sobriety and finding steady work pushed Dru to his limits. He moved again, eventually landing in Phoenix, Arizona.

In Phoenix, Dru's past caught up with him in a way he hadn't **anticipated**.

Set up by a **confidential informant**, he narrowly avoided a police raid. The experience shook him to his **core**, forcing him to confront the **reality** that he couldn't keep running from his past. Escaping the heat.

Determined to change, Dru left Phoenix and returned to Miami. There, he embraced the sun-soaked streets, finding **solace** in the warmth and rhythm of the city. But Miami's challenges persisted—language barriers and a lack of **opportunities** made it difficult to build a stable life.

After months of struggling, Dru returned to Colorado, ready to try again.

Dru's return to Arizona marked a turning point. Though he was arrested for a minor offense, the **elements** were getting to him—the heat and dehydration taking a toll. Dru wasn't thinking straight.

Approached by a police officer, he refused to comply. The officer called for backup, and during the apprehension, Dru found himself in a physical altercation with Phoenix's finest. Falsely arresting Dru while failing to read Dru his rights. he became a victim of **police misconduct**. A video **surveillance** tape shows his **innocence** yet they system failed to bring him **justice** making.

The arrest was embarrassing. People in the store asked,

"Why are you attacking him? He didn't do anything!" But their words did nothing to stop the cops.

The charges against Dru were **fictitious**. They stacked multiple charges on him, only to drop them all—except one: assault on an officer.

Seeing the **judge**, Dru was denied bail and offered a diversion program requiring anger management, which would have dropped all charges. The judge rejected the deal.

Dru had never been in trouble in Arizona before, yet he was never read his rights. He sat in jail for months, waiting for trial, until they finally offered him time served. With no other choice, Dru took the deal— hoping to appeal, but the request was denied.

CHAPTER 7

JOURNEY IN THE SYSTEM BEGAN

For Dru, being "in bound" within the **restrictions** of probation seemed like a trap designed to drain his spirit. Yet, he found an unexpected source of energy in those very **constraints**. Bound by Arizona's probation system, Dru realized that the limits **imposed** on him also gave him a unique focus. Without the ability to escape or run, he had no choice but to confront his circumstances head-on.

"I found more energy in being in bound than I ever did in being free," Dru reflected. "Freedom without direction is just another kind of prison."

Reading books was an outlet behind the walls, but not just any type of read. Dru used jail to learn from the old heads. He began preparing for a better future, but first, he had to understand his underlying issues—he had to forgive and forget. He befriended the old timers, giving them conversation in exchange for **knowledge**.

Being incarcerated is horrible, it's also a way to reserve and reflect on yourself—gain understanding and apply it.

Dru began to see his probation as a **framework** within which he could build something meaningful. While the rules and restrictions often felt **suffocating**, they also forced him to slow down and think **strategically**.

He used this time to **plan**, **prioritize**, and **focus** on the things that truly mattered.

Dru spent most of his free time on the streets and in the library, protesting for change. He had multiple run-ins with security guards and police officers. To protect himself, he would record the interactions. This **tactic** gave him a blanket of protection and made the cops submit—to a fervent extent.

They would **ban** Dru from libraries, parks, and train platforms, but he knew the law. He never gave his ID to police officers, so legally, they couldn't ban him. They were salty about Dru's understanding of the law and sometimes became physically aggressive with him.

Dru, doing the Bristol stomp through Arizona, keeping it true to himself, was used to police confrontation—so he never bowed down. He challenged the law back.

Counting down the days left in Arizona—it had been 10 months. Dru had been beating the Arizona system so far while maintaining 13 different **sources** of income. That was **assets** and **equity.**

Dru never had any **ownership** while hustling. He invested in the ladies and took major losses, knocking the wind out of his sails. But being **resilient**, he kept rebuilding until he found the right **algorithm** for himself.

When he found it, he began with finding **balance** in the stock market— strategically adding more investments and gaining his first ownerships of multiple entities. While maintaining his business, building his **credit**, and publishing books, a 35-year-old Dru was now taking his pain to another **level**. He **yearned** for **success** and got fuel from the hate the state provided.

To fund his stock and business, Dru worked for a media company, spinning signs and getting paid 1099 cash. He would transfer it to his business account—that's dirty money to clean.

The plan was not to get rich. Dru knew the stakes were way too high with the energy the cops provided. So, to be safe, he just used the business at this rate to keep it in good standing and to keep probation off his back.

It was working. Dru was a **genius.**

He found out he was **autistic**—that was the reason for most of his underlying issues.

Dru wrote in his journal:

"With great understanding, that's react and gains. Without understanding, that's a fact remains."

"The boundaries gave me clarity,"

Dru explained.

"They forced me to look at what I had, not what I was missing."

This shift in perspective allowed Dru to channel his energy into his business, investments, and **personal growth**. Every day became an **opportunity** to prove to himself that he could **thrive**, even under the weight of the system.

The constraints of probation demanded discipline, something Dru had struggled with in the past. But instead of resisting, he leaned into the structure, using it as a tool to **develop** better habits.

He created **routines** that kept him grounded: waking up early, setting goals for the day, and **dedicating** time to his business and investments.

"**Discipline** isn't about restriction," Dru realized. "It's about giving yourself the freedom to grow."

Each small act of discipline **reinforced** Dru's belief in his ability to **overcome**. Whether it was sticking to a budget, completing a task, or resisting **temptations**, every **victory** added to his **momentum.**

Being stuck in Arizona often felt **isolating**, but Dru found ways to turn that isolation into focus. Without the distractions of constant movement or **external** pressures, he had the space to think deeply about his goals and priorities.

The time he spent at the library, working on his business and investments, became a sanctuary of sorts. It was a place where he could escape the chaos of the streets and immerse himself in the future he was building.

"Sometimes, being in bound forces you to look inward," Dru said. "And that's where you find the strength to keep going."

Through his journey, Dru came to understand that the limitations imposed on him weren't just obstacles—they were opportunities for growth. Each constraint challenged him to think creatively, adapt, and find new ways to succeed.

The **energy** he found in being in **bound** became a driving

force, pushing him to achieve more than he ever thought possible.

In the strangest way, understanding the **system** gave Dru structure he never had. So, he's not against incarceration—just against a lack of encouragement.

If you're reading this behind the walls, this is a map to understanding
OPPRESSION.
DAT FEEL

At this age, Dru had done a world tour of county jails. His kids could Google him and see all his mugshots.

Dru felt that his only way to keep the peace with his kids was to make a manual.

SMART RECOVERY works only with understanding and applying the corrective actions. Removing vices and codependency is the biggest part of **SMART** recovery—also forgiving yourself for not understanding and then working on rebuilding your life one day at a time.

Dru wrote in his journal:

"Nothing out of nothing means nothing—something out of something means something."

Dru had been in and out of rooms, struggling to understand the purpose of trying to grasp a book designed to get you sober —when the author was under the influence.

That's contrary to sobriety. Dru had a different vision that most people couldn't understand, and the cops always singled him out—bullying him.

"Only thing worse than a coward is a coward with power," thought Dru.

He started recording all his encounters with the police just to save his **integrity**.

It worked.

The cops would change their tones and then respect Dru. That's **resilience**.

In his journal, Dru wrote:

> *"The system tried to hold me back, but all it did was show me how strong I really am. Sometimes, the greatest energy comes from the places you least expect."*

If you have 24 hours in a day and you sleep for 8 hours, work for 8 hours—what do you do with the remaining 8?

When Dru was doing **drugshabitually**, he would spend those extra hours in an emotional slump, not allowing his brain to grow—just age.

That's selfish.

Dru thought he wasn't using any of those hours to build his own solid foundation.

Time and space became his best strategy.

Dru didn't believe in **mental illness.** Instead, he sought **meditation** and figured out how to balance his **chakra**. He retrained himself to use both sides of his brain—on his own.

Dru isn't writing this in hopes that this method can help the reader. It's truly his **testimony**.

He suffered greatly and lost his mind—only to rebuild and

forget everything that schools taught. He found his own understanding.

The mind is a fragile organ and needs to be tempered to change.

If you apply these lessons, you may find a **silver lining** to your own issues.

Honesty is the key to change. Be true to thyself.

CHAPTER 8

EMERGING FROM SURVIVAL MODE

Dru had spent years surviving—living day-to-day in Arizona's system, **navigating**homelessness, and working tirelessly to build something out of nothing. But now, as his efforts began to bear fruit, he felt a shift.

Survival wasn't enough anymore. It was time to move beyond merely getting by and step into the spotlight of his potential.

"I've been surviving for too long," Dru reflected. "It's time to thrive." The transition wasn't immediate.

Dru had grown accustomed to the rhythm of survival, where every action was about making it through the next moment. Shifting his mindset to one of growth and opportunity required effort, discipline, and, most of all, belief in himself.

For Dru, belief was a fragile thing—something he had fought to protect despite a lifetime of setbacks. He clung to it now, nurturing it with every small victory and every step forward.

"If I can make it this far," he thought, "there's nothing stopping me from going further."

The business Dru had built from the library's public Wi-Fi was finally gaining traction. Small but steady profits began to flow in, and with each successful transaction, Dru's confidence grew. He reinvested every dollar, carefully balancing his resources between growing his business and expanding his stock portfolio.

Dru's days became a whirlwind of activity. Mornings were spent at the library, managing the logistics of his business. Afternoons were devoted to researching investments and tracking market trends. Evenings were for reflection, where he reviewed his progress and adjusted his goals.

"Succession planning was non-stop for Dru he was always creating ways to improve his situation."

Using the lessons he had learned from the streets, Dru operated with **precision**. His ability to adapt, **think critically**, and stay disciplined gave him an edge, even in a competitive market. He also began to explore new opportunities, branching out into areas he had only dreamed of before.

"My success isn't about luck," Dru often reminded himself. "It's about preparation meeting opportunity."

With growth came new challenges. Dru quickly realized that success brought its own set of pressures—managing clients, meeting deadlines, and navigating the **complexities** of **entrepreneurship** while still dealing with the constraints of probation.

One particularly difficult moment came when Dru had to turn down a **lucrative** opportunity because it required travel outside of Arizona. The restriction stung, a reminder of the system's lingering grip on his life. But instead of dwelling on the setback, Dru used it as motivation to push harder.

"I can't control everything," Dru thought. "But I can control how I respond."

Dru also faced skepticism from those around him. Some doubted his ability to succeed, while others questioned his motives.

"Why are you wasting time on this?" one acquaintance asked. "Why don't you just get a regular job?"

Dru didn't bother explaining himself. He knew that his path was unconventional, but it was his own.

"They don't need to understand," he told himself. "As long as I believe, that's all that matters."

One evening, while reviewing his accounts, Dru realized something incredible: for the first time, his combined business and investment earnings had surpassed $10,000. The milestone was more than just a number—it was a symbol of how far he had come.

"From sleeping on the streets to this," Dru thought, tears welling in his eyes. "I'm not just surviving anymore. I'm building something real."

He celebrated the moment quietly, knowing that his journey was far from over, but feeling a profound sense of pride in what he had accomplished. For Dru, this milestone was about more than money. It was proof that his efforts were paying off and that he was capable of creating a better life for himself.

Dru's success wasn't just about money. It was about creating a foundation for the future—one that he could pass on to his children. He began to think about legacy, reflecting on how his journey could inspire others to rise above their circumstances.

"I want my kids to know that no matter how hard life gets, you can always find a way forward," Dru said. "Your past doesn't define you—your choices define your past."

As Dru was a product of his environment, he started documenting his journey in greater detail, keeping journals filled with lessons, strategies, and reflections. These writings became a source of guidance not just for himself, but for those who might one day follow in his footsteps.

Dru also began mentoring others in his community, sharing his story and offering practical advice. Whether it was helping someone create a budget, guiding them through the basics of investing, or simply offering words of encouragement, Dru found fulfillment in giving back.

"Helping others reminds me of why I started this journey," Dru said. "It's not just about me—it's about making a difference."

As Dru's financial situation improved, he made a concerted effort to reconnect with his children. Phone calls turned into video chats, and he began planning for the day when he could be with them in person. He also reached out to his mother, seeking to mend their strained relationship.

"It's not about what happened before," Dru told her. "It's about what we do now."

Though the road to reconciliation wasn't easy, Dru's commitment to healing his family bonds reflected the growth he had achieved. He wanted to be not just a provider, but a source of strength and guidance for those he loved.

For Dru, reconnecting with his family wasn't just a personal goal—it was a way of honoring the resilience that had carried him through his darkest moments.

"They've been my reason to keep going," Dru said. "Now it's time to show them what's possible."

Looking back on his journey, Dru felt a deep sense of gratitude—for the lessons, the struggles, and the moments of triumph that had shaped him. He knew that his path had been anything but conventional, but it was his own, and he had walked it with courage and determination.

In his journal, he wrote:

"Success isn't just about what you achieve. It's about who you become in the process. And I've become someone I'm proud of."

Dru knew that the road ahead would still have challenges, but he felt ready to face them. Armed with the lessons of his past and the strength of his present, he looked forward to a future filled with possibility.

Dru was no longer in survival mode—he was now building and maintaining. The transition taught Dru humility and strength. During incarceration, Dru read a book in Somerset County Jail in New Jersey. The quote that stuck out the most was:

"The best bosses go through the hardest things in life."

Dru got out of jail and went to the streets, but the mission was different—it was school time. He then would push himself through difficult times just to be the best boss.

As Dru started earning more cash, his mission was to save everything and take it back to the East Coast to put his town on.

As the stakes got higher, he disguised himself as a bum—wearing the same clothes for days, keeping his shoes dirty, and letting his feet stink. He walked around and slept wherever he got tired. No one ever knew what Dru was cooking in his Apple phone.

He was so Bristol with the attitude, highly misunderstood to say the least. From time to time, he would compose beats and freestyle for folks on the train, creating jingles for his business.

Dru was a man of many talents. His grandma told him, "You need to be able to do at least ten things in life."

Dru traveled the world, learning each state's financial practices and street systems, then started implementing them in his life. Now, he was sharing the knowledge because it worked—with diligence and militant responses.

"Our brain is a processor, and we can train it to process anything with practice and repetition."

Dru's daily routine consisted of him using all free resources to manipulate the streets. He was broke, but he blended well—using Planet Fitness to shower and cut his hair. He started growing facial hair to give off that **Neanderthal** look. But he had a Bristol mindset.

CHAPTER 9

LESSONS FROM THE STREETS

Lessons were endless. On a regular day was 15 things happening at once.

Dru often described the streets as the harshest, yet most honest, teacher he'd ever encountered. Homelessness stripped away the **illusions** of **safety** and stability, forcing him to confront life in its rawest form. Every day was a battle for survival, and every night brought new challenges. Yet, within the chaos, Dru found moments of clarity—lessons that would shape the way he approached his future.

"The streets don't lie, they show you who you really are, as versus to the school they shape you for a political outlook killing your cognitive functions creating emotional beings" Dru often said. "That's modern-day slavery."

For Dru, homelessness wasn't just a physical state; it was a confrontation with himself. **Self-accountability**. The streets forced him to navigate not only external dangers but also the

internal battles he had avoided for so long. **Fear**, **shame**, and **anger** rose to the surface, demanding his attention. But with every challenge, Dru grew stronger, finding **resilience** in places he didn't know existed.

When Dru first found himself homeless, it was easy to blame the world for his situation. Learning the truth was the silver lining to Dru's recovery of drugs, **violence**, and **self-negligence.**

He told himself that the system was rigged, that people didn't care, and that his **circumstances** were beyond his control. But deep down, he knew there were problems he hadn't faced—wounds he hadn't healed.

"I wasn't just running from the world," Dru admitted. "I was running from myself."

At first, the streets seemed like an escape. There was no one to answer to, no expectations to meet. But this freedom was **deceptive**. Without responsibilities or accountability, Dru's days blurred together, filled with aimless wandering and fleeting distractions. He would drink, smoke to **disguise** his growth showing the other homeless folks he was just like them, and hustle to survive. It worked.

While yes, Dru's not perfect with a life of turmoil, the **drugs** are not the crutch of recovery.

"Not understanding your brain functions is the driver away from freedom."

Yet, no matter how busy he kept himself, the weight of his unresolved issues followed him.

One night, sitting on the curb outside a convenience store, Dru watched as people walked by, their lives seemingly intact and orderly. "I used to be like them," he thought. "What happened to me?"

The realization hit him like a punch: he wasn't running from others—he was running from the version of himself he had lost.

The reality of homelessness was far more uninviting than Dru had anticipated. He was now getting rich but in danger of dying at any moment. Finding a safe place to sleep was a nightly challenge. He often had to choose between the vulnerability of sleeping outside and the unpredictable dangers of overcrowded shelters. Food was scarce, and even the smallest comforts—a hot meal, clean clothes—felt like luxuries.

Dru vividly remembered one night when he slept in the doorway of an abandoned building. The cold seeped through his thin blanket, and the sounds of the city—sirens, footsteps, muffled arguments—kept him on edge.

"You learn to adapt quickly," Dru said. "But the streets don't give you time to feel sorry for yourself."

There were also moments of humiliation. Dru, being autistic with an IQ between Elon Musk and Albert Einstein, was misunderstood by people with low IQs. They would pick on and bully him verbally, trying to get him to snap and physically attack. Dru knew that the stakes were high, so he would intelligently respond to the bullies, causing confusion upon them. Dru would leave them stuck like a starfish.

Another time, he stood in line at a soup kitchen, only to have the food run out before it was his turn. Dru always kept food. He sat down at the soup kitchen and prepared himself a hoagie, showing the people his independence. They looked at Dru like he was outta place.

"DAT FEEL."

"These moments make you," Dru reflected. "They teach you that you're capable of surviving."

Despite the hardships, the streets taught Dru lessons he couldn't have learned anywhere else. Each experience, no matter how painful, shaped his perspective and deepened his understanding of life.

- Adaptability: Every day brought new challenges, from finding food to avoiding dangerous situations. Dru learned to think on his feet, to read people and environments with precision, and to stay one step ahead.
- Resourcefulness: With limited resources, Dru had to get creative. He found ways to stretch a dollar, repurpose discarded items, and even barter with others for essentials.
- Resilience: The streets tested Dru's limits, but they also showed him his strength. Surviving each day was a victory, a reminder that he could endure even the toughest circumstances
- Compassion: Homelessness introduced Dru to people from all walks of life—each with their own stories of struggle and survival. These encounters deepened his empathy and reminded him of the shared humanity that connected them all.
- Acceptance of Help: Dru had always prided himself on being independent, but the streets humbled him. Accepting help—from a stranger, a shelter, or a community program—taught him that strength isn't about doing everything alone.

- Consistency: Acting or done in the same way over time, especially so as to be fair or accurate.

Dru knew that staying consistent in his journey could and would breed success.

SMART Recovery is a fresh approach to addiction recovery. **SMART** stands for (Self-Management and Recovery Training).

This is more than an acronym: it is a transformative method of moving from addictive substances, negative behaviors, To a life of positive self-regard and willingness to change.

Far too many people feel powerless over their lives and carry a sense of futility, a dread of staying trapped within an addiction pattern and locked into their circumstances.

SMART helps them learn the skills they need to overcome their addictions and transform their lives.

SMART was created for people seeking a self-empowering way to overcome addictive problems.

What has emerged is an accessible method of recovery, one grounded in science and proven by more than a quarter-century of experience teaching practical tools that encourage lasting change.

SMART is a powerful recovery community that includes passionate volunteers who recovered with **SMART** who are driven to help others. Peers and professionals working together fuse science and experience to help people build healthy and balanced lives.

In our mutual support meetings, offered online and in-person, participants design and implement their **ownrecovery plan (your own story)** to create a more balanced, purposeful, fulfilling, and meaningful life.

SMART provides specialized meetings and resources for a variety of communities, including Family & Friends, veterans, and more.

SMART Recovery works. Whether an individual has chosen recovery as their path or been mandated to attend a recovery program, **SMART** provides a path to Life Beyond Addiction.

Evidence-Based Practice: **SMART Recovery** uses evidence-based methods, including cognitive-behavioral, non-confrontational motivational enhancement, and other methods. Our meetings focus on the application of these methods, as guided by **SMART** 4-Point Program

- **Building and Maintaining Motivation**,
- Coping with Urges,
- Managing Thoughts, Feelings, & Behaviors
- Living a Balanced Life.

The methods used in **SMART Recovery** evolve as scientific knowledge evolves.

It's okay to get help.

Learn, that all the help isn't designed to help. Some people help for a paycheck."

recalls a conversation he had with a guy who was getting help from the shelter. The man had been living there for 12 years. "They provide his shelter needs, but they were unable to help him obtain a residence outside the shelter's structured system."

"That man was disabled and probably is gonna keep getting help."

Dru realized that the shelter makes money to provide a bed and food, but they are not obligated to help you get stable housing.

He saw the trap. People were depleting away slowly.

"Free help is awesome," Dru thought. "But I'm paying a mental price to get it."

With the shelter full of drugs, guns, and violence, he looked around to see everyone celebrating daily, and people were dying as well.

After two months, Dru decided that he must leave the shelter if he wanted to thrive.

So he took a leap of faith.

The turning point came when Dru realized that no amount of running could fix the problems he was avoiding. The streets weren't a hiding place—**they were a mirror, reflecting back the parts of himself he didn't want to face**.

"I thought I could escape my pain by staying busy, by surviving," Dru reflected. "But the streets showed me that the only way out was through."

This realization didn't happen overnight. It was a gradual process, one shaped by countless moments of reflection and hard truths. Dru began journaling, using his words to process his emotions and confront his fears. He asked himself difficult questions.

"Why was I running?"

"What do I truly want from life?"

And most importantly—

"What am I willing to do to change?"

Dru's journey wasn't just about surviving—it was about **reclaiming** himself. He started making small but **deliberate** changes. He distanced himself from **destructive influences**, sought out knowledge, and embraced the discipline that would allow him to rebuild his life. Instead of numbing his thoughts with substances, he trained his mind to focus on growth.

Leaving the shelter was the hardest yet most necessary step. It wasn't just about escaping the chaos—it was about stepping into responsibility. Dru knew that if he wanted a different life, he had to create it himself.

The streets had taught him lessons no school ever could.

Dru didn't just walk away from homelessness.

He walked toward something greater.

CHAPTER 10

GET RICH OR DIE TRYING

Dru had always lived by one mantra: get rich or die trying. It was more than just a **motto**—it was his survival **mechanism**, a way to stay focused in a world that offered him no shortcuts, no handouts, and no guarantees.

But as the days turned into months, and the grind of the streets tested him in ways he never imagined, Dru began to realize that this mindset, while powerful, came with a cost.

"I thought getting rich was the only way to prove my worth," Dru reflected. "But what I didn't see was that survival itself was already a victory."

The streets demanded Dru's full attention. Every day was a test of his resourcefulness, patience, and determination. Dru began collecting coins as a form of stock—purchasing coins from the bank, and he would return the coins that had no value. During the course of these purchases, the bank accidentally gave

Dru a nickel instead of a quarter. Dru did not like that he was just shorted by the bank—an accident, but a mistake nonetheless.

Dru got even with the bank by purchasing multiple rolls of nickels as well as quarters. He began filling the coin rolls with quarter, nickel, quarter—only to match the same number of coins but to short the bank four dollars a roll. He would profit four dollars per roll, taking the proceeds and investing them in stocks, creating a free purchase.

And while his **mantra** kept him going, the challenges he faced forced him to redefine what wealth and **success** truly meant.

One day, Dru was walking along the Blade, selling cigarettes to scrape together a few dollars. He approached a local junkie, a man whose face bore the wear of years of addiction. The man handed Dru a tarnished 50- cent coin in exchange for a single cigarette. It was a small transaction, but to Dru, it felt **monumental**.

"That coin wasn't just payment," Dru said, turning it over in his hand.

"It was proof that I could create value, even when I had nothing."

Dru pocketed the coin and carried it with him everywhere. It became a symbol of his resilience, a reminder that even the smallest victories mattered. On days when he felt **overwhelmed** or defeated, he would pull out the coin and let its weight ground him. He would take it out and spin it— the sound gave him a confidence DAT FEEL.

"This little piece of metal kept me going," Dru said. "It reminded me

that no matter how small the win, it still counts."

Dru quickly learned that no one could help him in the way he truly needed. The world wasn't set up to carry people like him; it was designed to push them down. The only help Dru ever received came in the form of knowledge, and even that required him to ask the right questions and seek out the answers himself.

"No one gave me a blueprint," Dru said. "The only help I got was the kind that made me stronger, but I had to earn it."

He spent hours at the library, piecing together information about investments, business strategies, and personal development. He studied successful entrepreneurs, **dissecting** their **methods** and **adapting** them to his own circumstances. Every step forward was hard-won—the result of tireless effort and an unrelenting drive to succeed.

"I realized that knowledge was the most valuable thing anyone could give me," Dru said. "And it was up to me to use it."

Despite his relentless determination, the weight of survival began to wear on Dru. One night, after a particularly grueling day of walking miles in search of work, he found himself sitting alone in a park. The city lights shimmered in the distance, but they felt worlds away from the reality of his life.

Dru was missing family and Bristol.

"I felt like I was running on empty," Dru admitted. "I started to wonder if I was even capable of making it out."

The hunger **gnawed** at his stomach, and the cold wind bit through his thin jacket. He reached into his pocket and pulled out the 50-cent coin, holding it tightly in his hand. It was a small comfort, a reminder of the **progress** he had made. But in that moment, even the coin's weight couldn't ease the ache in his heart.

For the first time in a long while, Dru felt truly **defeated**. The get rich or die trying mindset that had once fueled him now felt like a **burden**, a constant reminder of how far he still had to go.

But Dru knew giving up was not an option. He had come too far.

He would go on YouTube to reflect on Bristol—to see his childhood friends gangbanging out of control. Kids were shooting without understanding morals. There were no positive outlets for Dru's town. With a sense of **urgency**, he began plotting ways to help his town as an entirety.

As Dru sat in the darkness, a memory surfaced—a piece of advice he had developed long ago: "Your circumstances don't define you. What you do with them does."

The words reignited something in Dru, a spark of determination that had been buried under layers of doubt and fatigue.

"I realized that no one was going to hand me the life I wanted," Dru said. "If I was going to make it, I had to keep pushing, no matter how hard it got."

From that moment on, Dru approached each day with **renewed focus**. He set small, achievable **goals**—finding a meal, earning enough to buy a notebook, and working on his business ideas whenever he had access to Wi-Fi. Each goal he achieved became a building block, a step closer to the life he envisioned.

Dru's journey taught him that true growth comes from within. While others could offer advice or point him in the right direction, the real work was his to do. He embraced this **truth**, using it to fuel his progress and strengthen his resolve.

"The only help I really needed was the kind that made me better," Dru said. "And that's the kind of help you have to earn."

He began to see his challenges as opportunities to learn and grow rather than as overwhelming obstacles. Each struggle was a chance to prove his resilience, test his limits, and build a stronger foundation for his future.

As Dru worked to rebuild his life, his definition of **wealth** began to shift. It wasn't just about money—it was about knowledge, resilience, and the ability to overcome obstacles.

"Real wealth is something no one can take from you," Dru reflected. "It's the skills you build, the lessons you learn, and the strength you gain from pushing through."

Mental freedom. DAT FEEL.

This new perspective gave Dru a sense of purpose that went beyond material success. He began to see his **journey** as a way to inspire others— to show them that even in the darkest moments, there is always a way forward.

Dru's efforts began to pay off. He used his earnings to invest in his business ideas, carefully researching each decision. He wasn't just surviving anymore—he was building a foundation for a better future.

Anticipation became a form of **anxiety** that Dru had to balance. Meditation was his source of relief—sitting alone, taking deep breaths, counting to ten, and slowly releasing each breath. Dru found inspiration in Tempe, Arizona, seeing how rich the views were. He could feel that he was getting closer to greatness.

Dru never panhandled; he always found positive **outlets** to pass the time. Unlike when he was growing up in Bristol—when his favorite pastime was violence, drugs, and **extortion**—he now reflected on how far he had come. It gave him a new blanket of hope.

He would watch seminars and learn how to prepare himself

for his business. Dru's biggest goal was to maintain and stay in **compliance**. He understood the emotional and logical scales of business planning and realized he possessed both qualities.

Succession planning was something Dru did daily. He was never bored—there was always something to do.

In the beginning, cash wasn't the chase. He was yearning for a solid foundation—one that could soon open doors for **juvenile delinquents** and **felons**, giving them a platform and a chance to serve their communities.

Dru did all this with the support of free resources, the church in Tempe being his biggest one, providing him with toiletries, clothes, and meals when he needed them most. The kindness he received from the church and local organizations humbled him. It made him realize that while **self-reliance** was his greatest strength, there was no shame in accepting help when it came with genuine intent.

Dru began volunteering at the church in return, stacking chairs after service, sweeping floors, and handing out food to others in need. It wasn't just about repaying the kindness—it was about being part of something bigger than himself. "Giving back made me feel like I had a place in the world," Dru admitted. "Like I wasn't just surviving anymore, but actually living with purpose."

As the weeks passed, Dru's focus sharpened. He developed a disciplined routine—morning meditation, reading financial books at the library, working side hustles, and journaling his thoughts. The streets had once dictated his every move, but now, he was taking control.

One evening, he sat on the steps of the shelter, looking out at the sunset over Tempe. The sky was streaked with shades of orange and purple, and for the first time in a long while, Dru felt a deep sense of **peace**. “I realized that success isn’t a **destination**,” he reflected.

"It’s the journey itself. Every lesson, every struggle, every small win—that’s what builds real wealth.”

Dru’s transformation wasn’t just financial—it was mental, emotional, and spiritual. He understood now that real success wasn’t just about getting rich. It was about breaking the **cycle**, creating something that lasted beyond himself. His dream of opening a business to help others—juvenile delinquents, felons, people who just needed a second chance—was no longer just a vision. It was a plan in motion.

With every step forward, Dru proved to himself that he was more than his past, more than his struggles. He was a builder, a strategist, a man on a mission.

“I used to think get rich or die trying was the only way,”Dru said, a small smile forming. “But now I see—live with purpose, and the wealth will follow.”

CHAPTER II

THE CLIMB TO STABILITY

The climb to stability for Dru was a **delicate** balance of understanding and managing his daily **endeavors**. He had learned to create mental checklists, marking off tasks as he accomplished them. Sobriety had been a turning point in his life, but it was far from the final destination. The deeper challenge lay in finding balance—a concept that felt foreign after years of chaos.

Dru's first year of sobriety had been foggy, a blur of just "**being**" rather than living with purpose. He remembered a time in New Jersey, working at CVS and living out of a hotel. He was new to his journey and excited about a fresh start. He'd just invested in the stock market, purchasing his first set of shares, hoping for a quick win. He put his whole check into it, but soon found himself in a bind. With no money left to pay for his room, he overdrafted his account. The next day, he was fired from his job, and as he stepped outside into a foot of snow, he wondered, "What now?"

A co-worker, seeing what had happened, pulled up in his car and offered Dru a ride back to the hotel, along with a life lesson that would stay with him:

"Sometimes, things fall apart to make way for something better."

His first year was often called "**the pink cloud**"—everything felt great at first, but then depression set in. His brain's **receptors** had been reset, leaving him feeling emotionally unstable. He realized that practicing gratitude was a major key to sobriety, and he often reminded himself, If you're reading this, be grateful you're alive and you have a chance to try again.

Self-care played a crucial role in recovery. Being selfish, in a way, meant focusing on staying clean, setting small goals that weren't focused on counting clean time, which could often become a **trigger** for **relapse**.

After years of poor decisions, rebuilding his life wouldn't be easy. "It's going to take time," he thought, "**but the end goal is to remove the substances and rebuild.**"

The practice of **SMART Recovery** was vital for Dru. It emphasized the importance of recognizing and identifying triggers. In his second year of sobriety, he kept refining his understanding of his **cognitive functions**— **memory**, **attention**, **decision-making**, and **reasoning**—all while working to reset his brain. It wasn't just about staying clean; it was about reconciling the ghosts of his past, building a meaningful present, and envisioning a hopeful future.

"Recovery isn't just about putting down the drugs," Dru reflected. "It's about figuring out how to stand when the ground beneath you feels shaky." **Reacclimating** to society only added to the weight. Dru felt like an outsider in a world that seemed to move too fast for someone who had spent years surviving day by day. The routines, expectations, and systems felt like **barriers**, not **bridges**. Still, Dru pressed forward, driven by a determination to rebuild himself.

During this time, Dru found an unexpected ally. She was someone who had her own battles to fight, someone who understood the struggle of trying to piece a life back together. She had left her home in search of clarity, only to find herself as lost as Dru. Together, they became each other's lifeline, navigating the rocky terrain of recovery with a bond forged in shared pain and mutual **hope**.

"She saw something in me," Dru thought. "And for the first time in a long time, I didn't feel so alone."

Their relationship was far from perfect. She struggled with anger issues, often lashing out at herself and the world around her. She had difficulty holding down jobs, her spirit fragile from years of disappointment and drug abuse. But Dru saw a spark in her—a resilience she didn't yet recognize in herself.

She was autistic just like Dru. "You're stronger than you think," Dru would tell her. "You just need to see it the way I do."

Finding strength in each other.

Dru took it upon himself to be a stabilizing force in her life, even as he worked to steady his own footing. When she doubted herself, he reminded her of the **progress** she had made. When her temper flared, he helped her channel that energy into something constructive. In return, her belief in Dru's vision gave him the encouragement he needed to keep moving forward.

"You're my mirror," Dru told her one evening as they shared a quiet moment. "When I see you fight, it makes me want to fight too."

Together, they started to dream of a future that was about more than just survival. They envisioned a life where their struggles could be transformed into lessons for others. They talked about starting programs for at-risk youth, creating spaces where people like them could find **guidance** and **support**.

While Dru found strength in his partnership, he couldn't escape the battles raging within himself. Sobriety forced him to confront the pain he had numbed for so long—the guilt of his past mistakes, the anger at the world's injustices, and the fear of failure. These emotions came in waves, often **overwhelming** him in the quiet hours of the night.

"There were times when I felt like I was drowning," Dru admitted.

"But I knew that giving in wasn't an option."

To cope, Dru turned to **meditation** and **puzzles**. It became his **sanctuary**, a space where he could sit with his thoughts without being consumed by them. Journaling, too, became a lifeline. Each word he wrote felt like a step toward healing, a way to **untangle** the web of emotions that had kept him trapped.

"Every time I put something on paper," Dru said, "it felt like I was taking back control."

Reentering society wasn't just a challenge—it was an uphill battle. Dru and his partner faced rejection at every turn, whether it was from employers who couldn't see past their histories or from systems that seemed designed to keep them stuck.

"Society isn't made for people like us," Dru thought. "But that doesn't mean we can't make a place for ourselves."

They struggled to find steady work, often taking odd jobs that barely covered their basic needs. The stress of constant uncertainty weighed heavily on both of them. There were days when Dru's partner would break down, questioning whether their efforts were worth it.

"You're not alone in this," Dru would tell her. "We're in this together, and we're going to figure it out."

One crisp morning, Dru and his partner woke up under the bridge where they had spent the night. The air was cold, and the hum of passing cars above served as a harsh reminder of their circumstances. Dru had developed a routine of checking his stocks every morning, even with their limited resources. His investments were a small but significant step toward building a better future. Sitting cross-legged on the damp ground, Dru pulled out his phone and logged into his trading app. As the screen loaded, he felt a familiar rush of **anticipation**. But when the numbers finally appeared, his heart skipped a beat.

"No way," Dru muttered, staring at the screen. His partner noticed his expression and sat up.

"What's going on?" she asked.

Dru turned the phone toward her, a slow smile spreading across his face. "It worked," he said. "The stock doubled. My method actually worked." Her eyes widened as she stared at the numbers.

"Are you serious?" she asked, her voice a mix of disbelief and excitement.

Dru nodded. "This is it. This is proof that what we're doing isn't for nothing."

For a moment, the weight of their reality lifted. They laughed and hugged, sharing a moment of joy that felt like a glimpse of the future they were working toward.

"This is just the beginning," Dru said. "We're not just surviving anymore. We're building something real."

As Dru reflected on how far they had come, he felt a deep sense of **gratitude**—not just for the progress they had made, but for the lessons they had learned along the way. The climb to stability was far from over, but Dru knew they were on the right path.

"We're not where we want to be yet," Dru said. "But we're not where we used to be. And for that, I'm thankful."

Stability for Dru wasn't defined by material things like houses, cars, or clothes—even though he'd earned some of those from his success.

Understanding and achieving **mental balance** was what gave him the stability to build a **foundation** for true success. Use this with further research on your own to create your own success by reshaping your steel (mind).

Dru sat in the park, staring at the ADP building. He noticed a group of homeless individuals nearby. As they approached him, recognizing him as an unfamiliar face, one of them asked if he had drugs for sale. Dru kindly turned them down and offered a life lesson instead.

"If you want drugs," Dru said with a wry smile, "the police station has plenty of drugs in evidence. Go there to purchase!"

The group chuckled, and Dru's words lingered in the air, a reminder that sometimes the most valuable currency in life wasn't money—it was **wisdom**.

CHAPTER 12

BREAKING FREE THE LAST CHAINS

By the time Dru reached this stage of his life, the chains holding him back were no longer **physical**. He had overcome addiction, endured homelessness, and navigated a justice system that seemed designed to trap him. Now, the chains were **internal**—the weight of **self-doubt**, lingering **trauma**, and the fear that his past might still define him.

"Freedom isn't just about escaping the system," Dru reflected. "It's about escaping the things you let hold you back." This chapter of Dru's journey wasn't about survival—it was about rediscovery. Breaking free wasn't a single moment of triumph; it was a process, built from small, deliberate steps forward.

Freedom for Dru wasn't a gift someone handed him—it was something he built, piece by piece, with his own two hands. Dru started a scrapping business, collecting and selling scrap metal to generate income. It wasn't glamorous, but it was his. He named the business **Expo Scrap Junk N Removal Services LLC**. Dru encourages the world to use his service as a tribute to his journey and the perseverance that had brought him to this point. Dru was the company's sole employee. He spent his mornings scouring neighborhoods, junkyards, and abandoned lots for scrap metal. It was physically demanding work—dirty and exhausting—but every piece he collected was a step closer to independence.

"I didn't care about the grime or the sweat," Dru said. "I cared about what it meant. Every load of scrap was proof that I could create something from nothing."

Dru's approach to running his business was unconventional but deeply personal. He paid himself **$14.87** an hour—not because he couldn't make more, but because it was enough to cover his bills, keep his business in good standing with the Arizona Corporate Commission, and satisfy his probation officer, who insisted he was mentally ill and fraudulent to the judicial system.

"It wasn't about the money," Dru explained. "It was about showing myself that I could earn my own way, even when the odds were stacked against me." By keeping his expenses low, Dru found a **sense** of **freedom** in **simplicity**. He didn't need luxury—just the knowledge that he was in control of his life.

"I was paying myself for being homeless," Dru said with a wry smile. "And learning. Because for me, freedom wasn't about having more. It was about doing things my way."

Running the scrapping business wasn't just a means of survival—it was a form of **resistance**. Every day, Dru would wake up before dawn underneath the bridge at Tempe Lake, from which he was banned multiple times by police officials. He challenged them anyway, learning the park hours and knowing when to go to sleep and when to wake up to avoid park rangers, cops, and passerby's. He created a routine in a caveman world, preventing his brain from shutting down, packing his tools into his backpack, and setting out to find the next haul. He navigated Phoenix's streets with a sharp eye, spotting value where others saw waste.

"Scrapping is about seeing potential where others see trash," Dru said. "And that's what I've been doing with my life all along."

The work wasn't without its challenges. There were days when Dru's body ached from hours of heavy lifting, and nights when he questioned whether it was all worth it. But each time he cashed in a load of scrap, he felt a renewed sense of purpose.

"It wasn't just metal I was collecting," Dru said. "It was pieces of my freedom."

As Dru's business grew, so did his desire to give back. He began mentoring at-risk youth, sharing his story and teaching them the skills he had learned along the way. Mentorship became a way for Dru to turn his pain into purpose. During a workshop at a local community center, a teenager asked him,

"Why didn't you just give up when things got hard?"

Dru smiled, pausing before he spoke. "Because giving up wasn't an option," he said. "Every time I wanted to quit, I remembered why I started. I wasn't just fighting for myself—I was fighting for the chance to prove that I could change."

These moments of connection reminded Dru that his journey wasn't just about him. It was about showing others that they could rewrite their own stories.

Dru's scrapping business wasn't the only way he worked toward freedom. He had also developed a habit of investing small amounts of money into the stock market. It wasn't much—

just a few dollars from each load of scrap— but Dru's disciplined approach began to pay off.

One morning, as Dru sat under the bridge where he often stayed, he checked his trading app and saw something that made his heart race.

"The stock doubled," Dru said, staring at his phone in disbelief. "My method actually worked."

He showed the screen to his partner, who had been on her own journey of recovery alongside him. Her eyes widened as she looked at the numbers.

"You did it," she said. "You're really making this work."

For Dru, the moment wasn't just about **financialsuccess**—it was about **validation**. It was proof that his hard work and **persistence** were paying off, even in small ways.

"This is just the beginning," Dru said. "We're not stuck here forever. We're building something real."

While Dru's business gave him a sense of purpose, the emotional work of breaking free was even harder. He had carried anger with him for years— anger at his parents, the system, and himself. Letting go of that anger was one of the most challenging steps in his journey.

"I realized my anger wasn't hurting anyone but me," Dru said. "Holding onto it was like carrying a burning coal in my hand."

Through meditation and therapy, Dru learned to release the resentment he had held for so long. He began to see forgiveness not as a weakness, but as a way to liberate himself from the past.

"Forgiveness isn't about letting people off the hook," Dru said. "It's about freeing yourself."

For Dru, freedom wasn't about material wealth or societal approval—it was about creating a life that reflected his values.

His scrapping business became a symbol of that freedom, a reminder that he could build something meaningful, even from the humblest beginnings.

"Freedom is doing what you want, even when the world tells you it's not enough," Dru reflected. "For me, this is enough."

As Dru looked back on his journey, he felt a profound sense of gratitude. Every challenge, every setback, and every small **victory** had shaped him into the person he was becoming. His scrapping business wasn't just a job—it was a **testament** to his resilience, **creativity**, and determination.

"Breaking free isn't about escaping your past," Dru said. "It's about using it to build something better." That's the result of redeveloping the brain and practicing **SMART Recovery**. Dru's main purpose wasn't to give the reader a bunch of crackly tales; he was more so trying to share how he got sober and successful from drugs.

CHAPTER 13

THE FIGHT FOR FREEDOM

The glow from Dru's phone screen illuminated his face as he stared at the numbers in disbelief. Red. Everything was red. His stomach tightened, and a lump formed in his throat as he swiped through his stock portfolio.

Another loss. Another investment gone wrong.

"Man, what's the point?" he muttered, tossing the phone onto his worn backpack. The echoes of past lessons from **mentors** and books felt distant now, drowned out by the crushing weight of his reality. Sitting under the familiar bridge, Dru pulled his knees to his chest, trying to shut out the world. But the cold air, the distant hum of traffic, and the chatter of nearby drifters wouldn't let him escape.

In that moment, Dru wasn't just facing a financial setback—he was grappling with something far deeper. The gnawing voice of self-doubt whispered, "Maybe you're just not meant to win."

Closing his eyes, Dru tried to quiet his thoughts. But instead of silence, memories flooded in—images of the old man he'd met in jail, the one who had planted the first seed of change.

"Every failure's a lesson, kid," the man had told him. "You only lose when you stop learning."

Back then, Dru hadn't understood the depth of those words. He had laughed them off, more focused on the chaos of his surroundings than the wisdom being offered. But now, years later, those words carried a new weight.

Dru opened his eyes and looked out at the streetlights flickering in the distance.

"Am I learning, or am I just losing?" he whispered.

The fight Dru faced wasn't one of fists or survival—it was one of endurance. It was about standing up to the invisible chains of fear, regret, and **hopelessness** that had kept him bound for so long.

The streets had taught him how to defend himself, how to survive. But this fight was different. This was a fight against himself.

"**Niagara Falls didn't start as a waterfall**," Dru said aloud, repeating a line he'd learned from the streets of Miami. "**It started as a trickle, carving through stone**." If water could carve stone, Dru thought, maybe he could carve his way through this life. But the question remained: How do I start?

As Dru sat there, the faces of those he had lost flashed before him. Friends who had **succumbed** to **overdoses**, family members broken by **alcoholism**, and even the kids who had grown up playing in the same parks where deals went down. The **epidemic** of addiction wasn't just about hard drugs—it was about everything that kept people trapped, from sugar to **self-doubt.**

Drugs killed my people, Dru thought bitterly. But it's not just the drugs you smoke or inject. It's the **habits**, the **vices**, the things that hold us back from becoming who we're meant to be.

He clenched his fists, anger rising in his chest. But this time, the anger wasn't directed outward. It was a fire within him, a burning desire to fight—**not just for himself, but for everyone still stuck in the cycle.**

Dru reached for his phone again, this time with a different mindset. He opened his stock portfolio and began **analyzing** his losses. Instead of wallowing in frustration, he asked himself: What went wrong?

As he reviewed his trades, patterns began to emerge. He realized he had been chasing quick wins, jumping on trends without doing proper research. He had let emotions drive his decisions instead of sticking to a plan.

"Okay," Dru said to himself, sitting up straighter. "Lesson learned. Time to do this the right way."

From that moment on, Dru approached the market with a new **perspective**. He started small, investing in stable companies and focusing on consistent growth. He embraced dollar-cost averaging, spreading his investments over time to reduce risk.

"Success isn't about avoiding losses," Dru realized. "It's about learning how to bounce back."

Dru began celebrating the small wins. A few dollars gained here, a stock price holding steady there—it wasn't much, but it was progress. He compared himself to a bird, gathering crumbs to build a nest.

"Crumbs add up," Dru said with a grin. "You don't need the whole loaf at once to survive."

These small victories gave him the strength to keep going,

even on the hardest days. They reminded him that progress wasn't always dramatic—it was steady, patient, and deliberate.

As Dru began to rebuild his **confidence**, he felt an overwhelming urge to share what he was learning with others. He thought of the young people he had mentored, the ones who looked to him for guidance.

"They need to know the truth," Dru thought. "Not just the wins, but the losses, too."

In his workshops, Dru started **incorporating** lessons about failure and resilience. He shared his own setbacks openly, showing his mentees that falling wasn't the end—it was part of the journey.

"Every loss is a step toward a win," Dru told them. "You don't lose when you fall. You lose when you stay down."

One of the hardest lessons Dru had to learn was about letting go—letting go of the habits, relationships, and beliefs that held him back. He called them "**vice grips**," the things that kept him stuck in place.

If it's holding you back, it's a vice, Dru told his **mentees**. And if you want to move forward, you've got to let it go.

For Dru, letting go wasn't just about quitting drugs or cutting ties with toxic people. It was about facing the fear of change and embracing the unknown. It was about believing that something better was possible, even when it felt out of reach.

Dru's journey in recovery had taught him the importance of **self-awareness** and honesty. Programs like **SMART Recovery** had shown him that progress came from within, not from external validation.

"Recovery isn't about being perfect," Dru said. "It's about

being honest with yourself and taking responsibility for your life."

He used the tools he had learned—meditation, reflection, and goal- setting—to stay grounded. And when the weight of the world felt too heavy, he reminded himself of his mantra: "**Progress, not perfection.**"

Dru's setbacks didn't define him—they refined him. Each loss, each mistake, each stumble was another step on the path to freedom.

As he looked ahead, he saw not just a future for himself, but for the people who depended on him.

This fight isn't just about me, Dru realized. It's about all of us. It's about showing that no matter how far you've fallen, you can rise again.

With renewed determination, Dru stood up, dusted himself off, and took the first step toward his next chapter.

A new kind of freedom. Dru sat atop a quiet hill, the city sprawling below him like a living, breathing map of his past. The evening breeze whispered through the trees, carrying with it the hum of car engines, the faint laughter of children, and the rustle of leaves.

This was his sanctuary, his place to reflect, to think, and to remember just how far he had come. For years, Dru had mistaken numbness for peace. He thought freedom could be found in distractions, in substances, or in fleeting escapes. But none of it had been real.

Freedom, Dru now realized, wasn't something external. It wasn't a destination, a person, or a prize to be won. True freedom was built brick by brick, through **resilience, reflection,** and the belief that life could— and would—get better. But the journey to this moment had been far from easy.

Dru's journey began with a single decision: **to take that first hit**. At just eleven, he had been lured by the promise of escape. His life was already filled with chaos—arguments at home, poverty pressing in on every side, and the constant noise of his own **insecurities**. Drugs seemed like an answer, even if he didn't fully understand the question.

He remembered the first time he smoked crack at a party. The air was thick with music, laughter, and the haze of smoke. A friend handed him the pipe with a grin.

"**This will take the edge off**," they promised. And for a moment, it did. The world blurred into something softer, something bearable. But that fleeting relief came at a price. Dru became a regular at those parties, the laughter and music masking the destruction happening inside him. By the time he realized he was hooked, it was too late. The drugs had seeped into every part of his life—his relationships, his schoolwork, his sense of self. He stopped caring about anything that didn't involve his next high.

Dru's addiction spiraled quickly. He began stealing to fund his habit— first from strangers, then from people he loved. He manipulated friends and family, making promises he knew he wouldn't keep. The guilt was suffocating, but the drugs drowned it out, at least **temporarily**.

One night, Dru found himself wandering the streets, **desperate** for a fix. He ended up at a dealer's house, surrounded by people he barely knew. The atmosphere was heavy with tension, everyone eyeing each other with suspicion. Dru's hands shook as he exchanged the last of his money for a small bag. He didn't care about the risks, the consequences, or the people around him. All he cared about was the next high, the fleeting escape that would momentarily quiet the chaos in his mind.

But as he walked away from the dealer's house, a cold emptiness settled in. For the first time in a long while, Dru felt utterly alone. The drugs had brought temporary relief, but they'd never filled the void inside him. He had traded everything—his **integrity**, his relationships, and his future—for something that only took more.

It was in that moment, standing on a street corner with the night closing in around him, that Dru realized the truth. He was drowning, not just in drugs, but in a cycle of self-destruction that had been years in the making.

The path to recovery wasn't easy, and there was no clear moment where everything changed. It was a slow, painful process of breaking down walls, confronting demons, and making choices that would, for once, benefit his future instead of his fleeting desires.

Dru found the courage to reach out for help. He joined a recovery program, and for the first time, he wasn't ashamed of his story. He learned to lean on others who had walked a similar path, who understood the struggles that seemed **insurmountable**.

It wasn't immediate, and there were days when the weight of the past threatened to crush him. But with each passing step, Dru found pieces of himself that he thought were long gone. He learned to forgive himself and to take responsibility for his actions without letting guilt hold him hostage.

Now, as Dru sat on the hill, watching the sun set over the city, he knew he had come a long way. His journey wasn't over, but he had learned that recovery wasn't about perfection—it was about **progress**. Each day he moved forward, no matter how small the step, was a victory. The pain of the past still lingered, but it no longer controlled him.

"Freedom isn't a destination," he said aloud to the quiet evening air. "It's a process. It's about making the decision to keep going, no matter how hard it gets."

Dru stood up and took a deep breath, feeling the cool night air fill his lungs. He wasn't the same person who had wandered the streets in search of his next high. He was stronger now, not because he had avoided the struggle, but because he had faced it head-on and kept moving forward.

With a renewed sense of purpose, Dru turned toward the future, ready to keep fighting for the freedom he knew was possible.

Mind of a murder started as an adolescent
our elders idols an og's molded us
cute with innocence , disguised us as a menace
misguided with ignorance, now our mind on a vengeance
but still can we keep our innocence?
Hatred as mental patrons
got us chasing pardons
going through jails symbolizing hell
standing tall In our cells
screaming fuck you to the wardens
but is society any different
mislead by the government
we was taught to kill and eat our own protein

we was poking shit as babies
growing up to slave for the monopoly
scruntized by the mid evil times
modernized by the worldy lies.
That's genicide
a vigorous ride, raised as gentle ones
that was molded to take no shit
a killer instinct Is not distinctive by the color of skin
pigmentation
but the pigs help change the nation
that's ventilation. no looney tunes
but now the rabbit got the guns and porky racing
it's bbq season.
Oppressed state of mind
pushed me through depressed day n times
and now the doc tryna prescribe me
compounds for my compromised mind
a natural way of living was designed
untainted until the dollar was symbolic
to the devil to pollute the nation
so without hesitation
we grew to out do each other
how fuck they call it United nation
98 percent of the world following each other
that means we have a huge shortage of leaders
we molded a nation to follow the leader
The leader is the number one feeder
for algae now we got remove of it
to get back to clear water
I mean clear order

monarchy was bc-ac, we in democracy
that's demolition
if I break it down it demo-racy
demolished the pure race and let's lead it with
pure fake
white out the black ink and smile like hooray
mind of a murder was formed from dismay
living in darkness granted death
from the carrier feelings were inferior trapped
in world of hysteria left a man weeping
from the reaping of what he sowed
asking the lord for forgiveness afraid of retaliation
from the road of sin
doing a little jail time freed himself within

The end ....

ABOUT THE AUTHOR

ART Kapone is a reformed individual who aims to inspire change in juvenile delinquents. Through personal experiences with drug addiction and crime, Art now mentors and educates others on substance abuse recovery and finding success.

www.ingramcontent.com/pod-product-compliance
Lightning Source LLC
LaVergne TN
LVHW041126150826
845673LV00007B/2192

* 9 7 9 8 8 9 6 9 1 4 9 7 6 *